For my husband, David

Many thanks to my parents, my sister Suzee,
and the vagabond cats on Gum Street.

Text and illustrations copyright © 2018 by Laura Lee

First Edition 2018

Library of Congress Control Number 2018930234
ISBN 978-0-9990249-4-2

2 4 6 8 10 9 7 5 3 1
Printed in China

This book was typeset in Muli.
The illustrations were rendered in Copic Multiliner pens with Digital Color.

Cover and title page lettering by Carrie Chan.
Brush used: Anna Mason by Rosemary & Co. round size 3
Paint: Moon Palace sumi ink
Carrie Chan's website is: aperfectsomething.com

Ripple Grove
Press

Portland, Oregon
RippleGrovePress.com

Thank you for reading.

cat eyes

laura lee

Ripple Grove
Press

In a world filled with many wonderful things,

Miki only sees cats.

At the start of springtime,

she spots cats at the neighborhood park.

Miki spies cats down busy streets

and tucked away among the tall buildings.

When it's raining,

cats escape underground.

And in sweltering summer heat,

cats stay cool down by the sea.

When autumn arrives,

cats take a seat at the back of Mrs. Shelby's class.

And they all come prepared for trick-or-treats!

Nobody seems to notice what Miki sees . . .

"Eat your peas," says Mom.

. . . that she really has cats on her mind!

"Bedtime!" calls Dad.

Just as Miki snuggles up with her favorite book . . .

. . . her adventure is cut short.

"Lights out!" say her parents.

That night, Miki dreams a marvelous dream . . .

. . . which she thinks about all the next day.

But when spring comes once again,

Miki's cats are gone.

Until one seemingly unspectacular day,

something special arrives.

"Hello," says Miki.

"Meow," says the cat.

Miki finally meets a friend

of her very own.

And then . . .